MARV

AND THE
BLIZZARD
ZONE

DEAR READER,

In this story, Marvin and his friends are ice skating at the Blizzard Zone. Ice skating is one of the most exciting things you can do, but it can also be a bit scary. Especially if, like Marvin's best friend Joe, you've not been out on the ice before.

I'm pretty bad at ice skating. Well, 'pretty bad' might be an understatement; every time I get on the ice my legs slip and slide in all directions, and I always end up falling painfully onto my bum at least a few times. However, I still go to ice rinks. I even still have fun at ice rinks. I guess you're wondering how. The answer to this great mystery is simple. It's because I always go to ice rinks with my friends. Friends have the great superpower to make things fun!

Sometimes it's easy to forget about this superpower. You might be too embarrassed or shy to join in or so eager to show off on the ice that you speed off and leave your friends behind, but you might be speeding away from all the fun too.

Marvin learns in this book, not to take the superpower of friendship for granted, and I hope that's something you can take away from it too.

Alex

That's me!

For my cats Akira and Simone – A.F-K

For SUPER YOU, the completely marvellous reader – P.B

OXFORD
UNIVERSITY PRESS

Great Clarendon Street, Oxford OX2 6DP

Oxford University Press is a department of the University of Oxford.
It furthers the University's objective of excellence in research, scholarship,
and education by publishing worldwide. Oxford is a registered trade mark
of Oxford University Press in the UK and in certain other countries

British Library Cataloguing in Publication Data

Data available

ISBN: 978-0-19-278048-5

1 3 5 7 9 10 8 6 4 2

Printed in China

Paper used in the production of this book is a natural,
recyclable product made from wood grown in sustainable forests.
The manufacturing process conforms to the environmental
regulations of the country of origin.

MARV

AND THE
BLIZZARD
ZONE

WRITTEN BY
ALEX FALASE-KOYA

PICTURES BY
PAULA BOWLES

OXFORD
UNIVERSITY PRESS

CHAPTER 1

Marvin and his best friend, Joe, couldn't sit still. The bus swayed around street corners and its engine made the seats rumble, but that wasn't the only reason they were fidgeting. Marvin and Joe were super excited because they were on their way to the Blizzard Zone!

Marvin had seen an advert for the
ice rink in Grandad's newspaper and had
asked if they could go. Grandad had said
yes, but they'd have to wait until the school
holidays, and so here they were, on the
first day of the holidays, on their way to
the best ice
rink in

the country! Grandad sat behind Marvin and Joe, playing a word game on his phone.

'So, what're you most excited for at the ice rink?' Joe nudged Marvin as he asked the question.

Marvin gave it some careful thought.

'Just . . . everything!'

Joe nodded, thinking hard. 'For me it's got to be the light show.'

Marvin thought back to the advert showing a huge number of lights shooting out in different directions on to the ice rink, in every colour of the rainbow.

'That will be really fun, but—'

'OK, maybe the music will be your favourite,' Joe interrupted.

Marvin shook his head. 'I don't think that's what I'm most excited for. I think I'm just excited to get out on the ice!'

This wasn't the first time Marvin had gone ice skating. He'd been a couple of times before and it had been a lot of fun.

'Ice skating?' Joe said, as though he hadn't even considered they'd be skating. 'Oh, yeah, we're going to be ice skating.' His face suddenly got all screwed up and serious. This would be Joe's first trip to an ice rink.

'Don't worry. It's not as hard as you think,' Marvin said.

'But what if I fall?' Joe said in a small voice.

'The first time I went skating I used a big plastic penguin to lean on and help keep my balance, but after that I just took a chance. Falling down and looking silly is all part of the fun!' Marvin mimed falling over in his seat and Joe laughed.

'Yeah, I guess that *is* part of the fun,' Joe said with a smile. They were best friends—who cared if Joe looked a little silly in front of his best friend.

Suddenly Marvin heard the sound of a faint high-pitched beeping coming from his bag. He ducked down, almost putting his whole head into the backpack. A small silvery face met his.

It was Pixel, Marvin's robot sidekick.
Marvin also had a super-suit which
transformed him into a superhero
called Marv. He took the super-suit
and Pixel everywhere with him, 'just
in case', as his grandad would say, but
it was important to keep Pixel and his
superhero identity hidden. Grandad
was the only person who knew Marvin's
superhero identity.

'I apologize for beeping. A sudden increase of excitement levels in my circuitry has temporarily broken my beeping functionality,' Pixel said.

'That's OK,' Marvin whispered.

'I believe you could help me fix the problem by taking me out onto the ice,' Pixel said. 'What's the human word? Please? Could you please take me ice skating?'

Marvin grinned at Pixel but before he could answer, Joe was hopping up and down in his seat again. 'Marvin! We forgot to even mention the hot dogs! Are you going to have onions on yours?'

'Pixel, I have to go, we'll talk about it later,' Marvin whispered.

Pixel bleeped disappointedly and slid back down into the backpack.

A couple of minutes later the bus slowly rumbled to a stop.

'Come on, we're here,' Marvin's grandad said, getting to his feet.

'Thank you, driver!' Marvin and Joe called out in unison as they hopped off the bus.

A cold breeze whistled past. Marvin and Joe zipped up their winter jackets. Ahead, covered in bright lights, was the ice rink. Marvin's face lit up.

'It's finally the school holidays,' Marvin said, quietly at first. It hadn't really sunk in until right now. 'It's the holidays!' Marvin said, louder this time.

'Whoop!' Joe cheered.

'Yes, it is indeed the holidays, now let's go get your skates and enjoy it,' Grandad said, giving them a wink. They headed to reception to grab some skates and then found somewhere to sit and put them on, while Grandad joined the queue for hot chocolate.

Joe was having a little bit of trouble putting on his skates, so Marvin helped him. He was concentrating so hard that it took him a while to realize that someone was calling his name.

'Hey, Marvin!'

Marvin turned to look and a smile sprung onto his face. It was Eva, from his class. She was smiling too.

'I didn't know you and Joe were going to be here,' she said.

'I didn't know you were going be here either,' Marvin said.

'Aww, look at how cute your little friends are, Eva,' a tall girl said, walking over to Eva and slinging an arm around her shoulders. Marvin's cheeks felt hot. He wasn't *that* little. Marvin looked up at the tall girl. Something about her was familiar. Marvin looked at Eva, then back at the older girl and then it hit him—they must be sisters! Behind Eva's big sister were a couple of her friends. They were all wearing ice skates. None of them had the usual plain white skates you borrowed from the ice rink. These

were much cooler. Eva's sister's skates
were blue with lightning bolts across
the sides. Marvin guessed they must be
really good at skating.

'This is my sister Ally, please just
ignore her.' Eva rolled her eyes.

'Do you three need some help getting
onto the ice?' Ally asked.

'No, why would you say that?' Marvin
frowned.

'Well . . .' Ally nodded to Joe.

Joe was trying to stand up on his
skates but as soon as he got up he
wobbled a bit and then fell back down
onto his seat.

Eva wasn't doing much better. She had put her skates on the wrong feet.

'Are you sure? I don't fancy your chances out there!' Ally said, laughing.

'We can skate just fine without any help,' Marvin snapped.

'Suit yourself.' Ally shrugged and turned to her friends. 'Come on, let's go. We're not wanted here. Probably for the best anyway, they're too slow to skate with us, and they'll be too scared to try out any of our tricks.'

Too scared? Marvin's eyebrows lifted. Did she really think he was too scared to skate with them? How could that be? Marvin was a superhero after all. He had defeated villains, chased down dinosaurs, and fought robot sharks. If only they knew what he was capable of. Everyone knew Marv the superhero was brave, but they didn't seem to see Marvin, the boy behind the super-suit. In their eyes, Marvin was just a little kid.

Marvin didn't like that. He had to prove them wrong.

CHAPTER 2

Marvin had to show Ally and her friends that he could skate just as well as them, and the only place to do that was out on the ice. Marvin stood up to go and felt a tug at his trouser leg. It was Joe.

'What was that thing that you were talking about on the bus?' Joe asked.

'What thing?' Marvin asked, impatient to get on the ice.

'The thing that helped you keep your balance the first time you went ice skating.'

Marvin scratched his chin, thinking. 'Oh, do you mean the penguins?'

Joe's eyes lit up. 'Yes! Can you please help me walk over to the reception and ask for one?'

Marvin groaned. He desperately wanted to go and skate but he also knew that he had to help his friend.

'Yeah, sure,' he said, with a sigh. 'Back in a minute,' he told Eva, who was now busy putting her skates on the right feet.

Marvin let Joe lean on him as they walked over to the reception. Marvin kept glancing back to Ally and her friends. They had already started skating around the rink. As soon as Marvin had helped Joe reach the reception desk, he left his friend and headed straight for the rink. But before he could get there, he heard a familiar high-pitched beeping sound coming from his backpack. Marvin grabbed the bag and found a quiet corner before opening it. Pixel's round head poked out.

'What is it, Pixel?' Marvin asked. 'I want to get out on the ice.'

'You said we'd talk about it later,' Pixel said.

'Talk about what later?'

A small square speaker extended out of Pixel's chest.

'Could you please take me ice skating?' a recording of Pixel's voice said.

'Pixel, I have to go, we'll talk about it later,' a recording of Marvin's voice replied.

'Wait, are you recording everything we say?' Marvin asked.

'Only since that one time you accused me of eating the last cookie when it was actually you.' Pixel crossed her arms grumpily.

'I did not eat the last cookie!'

'Well I'm a robot. I don't even eat cookies,' Pixel said. 'Anyway. Can I please go skating with you? It sounds so, so, so exciting—and I'm sure there's some useful superhero data I can gather over there on the ice.'

Marvin looked over to where Pixel

was pointing. His eyes went wide. Ally and her friends were already doing tricks out on the ice.

Marvin dropped his backpack.

'Ouch!' Pixel yelped as she hit the floor, but Marvin wasn't listening. He set off towards the entrance to the ice rink.

'Where are you rushing off to?' Grandad suddenly stepped in front of him and Marvin skidded to a halt.

'I just want to do some skating,' Marvin said with a shrug.

'Sure,' Grandad nodded. 'But remember why we came here.'

'To skate, I know.' Marvin tried to wave him away but Grandad simply shook his head.

'I'm here to drink many cups of hot chocolate, and you're here to have fun with your friend.' Grandad sighed. 'I've seen you rushing around. It's not a race you know. There's no competition here.'

'I know,' Marvin said as he glanced over his shoulder. Joe was slowly hobbling towards him, pushing the plastic penguin. Eva was at his side helping him along. 'Joe can meet me on the ice when he's ready. I just want to get out there and make the most of today.'

Grandad stepped to one side. 'All right, but remember what I said, OK?'

'OK, Grandad. I will.' Marvin walked past his grandad and finally reached the ice.

His first couple of steps were unsteady but with each passing moment, his memory of what to do came back to him. Soon Marvin was skating forward, zipping around the ice rink. But he wasn't fast enough. Up ahead he could see the older kids skating. It looked as though they were moving so effortlessly.

'Woooah!' Marvin heard Joe cry out. He glanced behind him. Joe was desperately clinging to his penguin as he slowly skated forward. Meanwhile, Eva was over at the side of the ice rink, holding tight to the barrier. Her legs kept slipping this way and that way, threatening

to dump her onto the cold ice. Joe and Eva glanced at each other and then burst out laughing at each other's wobbles. Laughing so hard made them almost fall and almost falling made them laugh even harder.

Marvin frowned. Part of him wanted to turn around and have fun with them, but he couldn't stop now. He had to prove to the older kids that he could skate. He concentrated as hard as he could, skating faster and faster, and swerving around people with ease. Marvin caught the attention of Ally and her friends and they even gave him a small round of applause as he skated in their direction.

Then all of a sudden music came
blasting into the arena and bright lights
flooded down from above. A rainbow
of colour danced around the ice rink.
Marvin stopped for a moment and looked
up in awe. It was a magical sight.

Just as Marvin started skating again, he heard Joe behind him.

'Marvin! Slow down!'

'Wait for us!' Eva called.

But Marvin didn't slow down. He was moving forward towards Ally and her friends.

'Hey Martin or Marvin, or whatever, you wanna skate with us for a while?' Ally called to him.

Marvin skated up to Ally and her friends, grinning. Almost as soon as he reached them, they all began to show off.

One girl spun around in a circle, quickly becoming a blur.

Another boy ducked down and whizzed through his friend's legs.

Marvin's jaw dropped. He hadn't seen anyone do moves like these before.

Then Ally skated forward. She pumped her legs really quickly to gather speed and then she leapt up into the air.

'Whoa,' Marvin whispered as Ally spun around 360 degrees in the air before landing back down onto the ice and skating onwards as if nothing had happened. Ally cast a lazy look in Marvin's direction and then waved him

forward. She didn't even have to say anything—Marvin knew what he had to do.

Marvin concentrated hard and tried to do exactly the same move as Ally. He pumped his legs as hard as could, shooting himself forward. Then he crouched down before jumping up with all his might. He did it! Time seemed to slow down when he was in the air. Marvin could see everything and everyone as if in slow motion—even Eva and Joe, who had caught up to him and the older kids.

Then time started moving at normal speed again, as Marvin began to fall. He hadn't even thought about landing! The ice rink around him became a blur as he tumbled down and then hit the ice. His legs skidded straight out from under him and he slid uncontrollably across the ice, crashing into Eva and Joe. They tumbled together into a great heap of arms and legs, with Joe's penguin on top of them all.

Marvin looked up to see the older kids laughing at them. The hot feeling he had felt earlier was nothing compared to this. Just when he had the chance to show everyone what a great skater he was, he'd messed it up!

Eva, Joe, and Marvin slowly untangled themselves from each other and began to get to their feet. Ally and her friends skated over to help them. Ally extended her arm for Marvin to take, but he shook his head. It was embarrassing enough to fall, let alone needing help to get back up.

Before Marvin could get to his feet, the music in the rink suddenly stopped and all the lights turned off, except for one spotlight focussed on the middle of the ice. All the skaters stopped what they were doing and turned to look. At first, Marvin thought it was part of the show, but that feeling didn't last long.

A boy in a glittering
skate suit glided
elegantly into the spotlight.
He clapped his hands
once—immediately grabbing
everyone's attention—and then
struck a dramatic pose.

'Behold! It's me—Master Blaster!' he said. 'I've seen quite a few awful skaters out here today so you know what? I think I should show you how this is really done.'

The crowd around Master Blaster began to murmur and mutter, unsure of what was going on.

'You all heard what I said. Shoo! Get off the ice and watch me perform.'

The other skaters began to look annoyed. Who did this skater think he was?!

'This seems like the right time for a superhero to butt in and save the day,' Joe said.

'Really? He seems harmless. He just wants to skate.' Marvin shrugged.

'Are you sure about that?' Eva asked.

'Boo! Get off the ice!' someone in the crowd yelled.

Master Blaster spun around on his heels and pointed at the person who yelled. An ice beam shot out of his hand and froze the person solid.

The crowd began to scream and run.

'You know what?' Marvin sighed. 'Maybe this is worse than I thought.'

CHAPTER 3

The crowd had scattered across the arena. Ice beams blasted across the rink, freezing people to the spot. Marvin used the chaos as a cover to quickly skate off the ice and find his backpack.

Marvin hid beneath the counter at reception to pull on his super-suit. It was time to become a superhero!

The only problem was that Pixel seemed unusually quiet. Normally by now her supervillain alarm would have been activated, but it hadn't.

Marv reached into his backpack and pulled Pixel out of the bag. She just hung there, limply. It was like someone had turned her off. Marv didn't know Pixel could be turned off!

Just then, an ice beam clanged off the reception desk. It was time to get a closer look at the situation. Marv peeked over the counter. Most of the people on the ice rink had been frozen solid. They were dotted around the arena like statues and Master Blaster was still firing!

'I've asked you nicely! If you won't settle down and pay attention, then I'll just have to force you to watch me as my ice statue audience! Ha ha ha!' Master Blaster's voice boomed.

Marv put Pixel carefully back in his backpack and rushed over to where he had left his grandad. When he got there, Grandad was sat at a table, frozen solid, with a still-warm cup of hot chocolate close to his lips. He hadn't even got a chance to taste it!

'Grandad, I promise I'll fix this and

get you and everyone else unfrozen.'
Marv glanced from his grandad's face to
the steaming cup. 'Hopefully, before your
hot chocolate gets cold.'

'Marv! Help!' Joe was calling him from the ice. Marv turned towards the ice rink. Was Joe still out there?

Marv knew he was going to need some powers if he was going to sort out this mess. He placed a hand over the 'M' on his suit.

'It's super-suit time! Super-suit, please activate super skates!' Marv said, and on cue his boots turned into a set of super cool rocket-powered ice skates.

As quick as a flash, Marv whizzed back onto the ice. The last time he'd been on the ice, he'd been a bit wobbly and it had taken all his concentration to try and keep up with the older kids. Now it was all so easy, he didn't even have to try to keep his balance. He was moving way faster than he'd

ever skated before. If it hadn't been for the supervillain freezing everyone in sight, it would've been a lot of fun.

Marv spotted Eva and Joe crouched behind Joe's penguin. They were the only people left on the ice who hadn't been frozen.

'Grab onto the penguin!' Marv yelled to Eva and Joe. They held onto it tightly and Marv burst forwards grabbing the penguin and pushing them over to the side of the ice rink so they could get off the ice.

'You should be all right now. Just stay here until—' Marv didn't get the chance to finish.

'Until what?' Master Blaster boomed from the centre of the ice rink. 'You think you can stop me?'

'Yeah, that's what I was hoping,' Marv replied.

'Well, come on then! Try it!' Master Blaster lifted his ice blasting arm and aimed right at Marv.

CHAPTER 4

'**F**REEZE!' boomed Master Blaster, firing a stream of ice towards Marv.

Quick as a flash, Marv dodged the incoming ice blast and went on the attack, skating hard towards the supervillain. But Master Blaster was too fast and too tricksy. He sped away, weaving through the frozen skaters on the rink. Whenever Marv thought he was catching up, Master Blaster would rattle off a bunch of ice beams which slowed Marv down. Soon the ice beams were coming fast and furious.

They buzzed past
Marv at speed, some
just missing his
shoulders and some
blasting right through
the space between his
legs.

'Why are you doing this?!' Marv
yelled at the villain.

'Because I wanted everyone to watch
me skate! What's the point of being
good at skating if no one
knows how brilliant I
am?!' Master Blaster
snapped.

'But that's just showing off,' Marv said, even though what Master Blaster said had sounded a little familiar.

Marv thought about how he'd acted earlier. All he'd cared about was showing Ally and her friends how well he could skate. He'd hardly spent any time with Eva and Joe. To his horror, Marv realized

he'd been acting just like a supervillain and it hadn't been much fun. Marv needed to apologize to Joe and Eva, but he had a supervillain to defeat first.

Suddenly, Marv heard Eva shouting from the side of the rink. 'Marv! Look at his necklace!'

Marv looked closely at Master Blaster. A glowing crystal dangled from a chain around the supervillain's neck. Maybe it was the source of Master Blaster's powers? Marv felt as though this might be the key to beating the villain but there was no chance of him even getting near to it right now. Master Blaster was still firing ice beams at him whenever he got too close.

What Marv needed right now was a sidekick. He needed Pixel. He skated over to his backpack but couldn't see any sign of her. And he couldn't wait around either, a couple of well-placed ice beams from Master Blaster kept him moving.

'I could really do with some help. I could really do with you, Pixel!' Marv yelled. It was the only thing he could think of doing.

Why wasn't Pixel out here helping him? Marv asked himself but deep down he already knew the answer. He took a deep breath and hoped that Pixel would hear what he said next.

'Pixel, I'm sorry,' Marv shouted. 'I

wanted to prove that I could be brave without the super-suit but I just ended up being a show-off. I've acted like a supervillain, not a superhero. And worst of all, I ignored you.'

'Who are you calling for?' Master Blaster said as he glided menacingly towards Marv. 'Do you really think anyone here could actually help you beat me?'

'Yes, I do,' Marv said. Despite having Master Blaster's hand aimed at him again, he stood his ground. 'Pixel can you help me? Please?'

'I thought you'd never ask!' Pixel whirred into action from the side of the rink, zooming over to Marv. Master

Blaster watched the reunion with a scowl on his face.

'Thank you, Pixel,' Marv said. His eyes were a bit watery and his chest felt full. 'I promise, Pixel, I'll never take our friendship for granted again.'

Pixel beeped so loudly that she was practically vibrating with joy.

'Sorry, lost control of my beeping functionality again. Apology accepted,' Pixel said.

'Oh really? I was just about to take care of one of you super losers, and now another has popped up out of nowhere. A robot this time.' Master Blaster stomped his skates on the ice and growled.

'Why can't you all just do as you're told? Stay still and watch me skate!'

Marv and Pixel shared a look.

'It's time to introduce you to my own super sidekicks . . .' Master Blaster struck a dramatic ice skating pose then clapped his hands. 'RELEASE THE PENGUINS!'

CHAPTER 5

The crystal in Master Blaster's necklace began to glow brighter and brighter. So bright in fact, that Marv could barely see the supervillain's neck and face, just Master Blaster's arms waving wildly around his head.

Marv caught a glimpse of movement out of the corner of his eye and turned to see a penguin. It was the one Joe had been using to skate, but somehow it was moving on its own.

It wasn't just that penguin either— every single penguin in the ice rink was coming to life and waddling forward.

They looked different now—on each of
their faces was a long, curly moustache.

Marv didn't know what to do and
watched, stunned, as the penguins
whizzed around the ice rink picking
up all the frozen statues of people and
plopping them around the edge of the
ice rink.

As soon as Marv was distracted, the villain summoned up his biggest ice blast yet. Marv only noticed something was wrong when a long shadow fell over him. He turned to see an avalanche of snow and ice looming above, ready to crash down.

'That's not good,' Marv said, sliding back.

'I don't know if I want to be on the ice any more,' Pixel bleated.

They tried to whizz away from the wave of snow, but they were too slow. It crashed down onto Marv and Pixel, burying them completely.

'Now that we've got that pesky superhero out of the way, it's time to complete my plan,' Master Blaster cackled.

'Pixel, are you OK?' shouted Marv from within the snow dump.

'Yes, but g-g-getting a bit c-c-cold. Could you get us out of here, Marv? P-P-Please?'

Marv tried to move but he was trapped in the ice and snow. He needed another superpower if he was going to break free and save the day, but which one? Marv closed his eyes tight and thought hard. His imagination whirred into action, and then he figured it out!

Marv's super-suit made a bunch of cracking sounds as small vents opened on its surface. Steaming hot air hissed out of the vents, melting the snow. In just a moment, it was gone, and Marv and Pixel were free!

'Th-thanks, M-M-Marv. I th-thought I w-was g-going to f-f-freeze.' Pixel shivered, moving closer to Marv's arm so she could warm herself on the vents in his suit.

Marv looked around to see a frozen crowd of skaters in front of him. The penguins had arranged them into an audience, just for Master Blaster's amusement.

'Supervillain detected! Supervillain detected! Supervillain detected!' Pixel cried.

'I'm so glad to hear you say that. I thought I'd never hear it again,' Marv said with a grin. 'Now the only question is, how do we stop him?'

'Based on the penguins' movement speed I estimate that in three minutes and twenty-three seconds, they will have finished moving everyone. And after that. . .' Pixel said.

'They'll be coming after us. Right?'

Marv frowned a little. They didn't have that much time. 'All right, it's time for a plan.' Marv and Pixel huddled together. They whispered for a couple of seconds before stepping back and giving each other a big high five.

Pixel jumped up onto Marv's shoulder and clung to his super-suit. Then Marv began to skate towards Master Blaster. The villain was busy giving a speech to the audience of frozen skaters, about his performance.

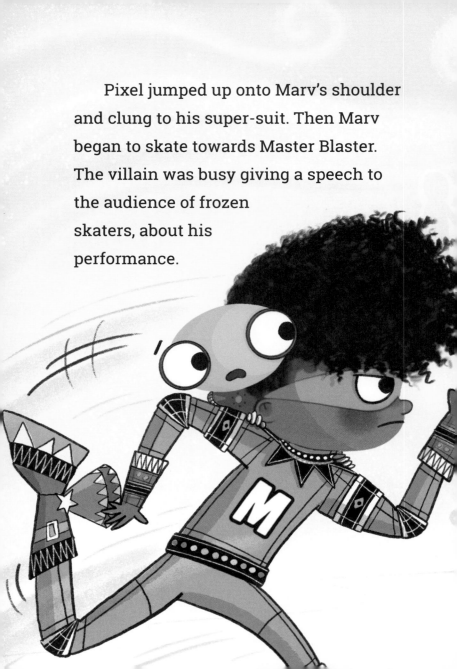

'Hold on tight, Pixel!' Marv yelled, as he began to pick up speed. Cold air rushed past them as Marv skated faster and faster.

'Are you sure this is going to work?!' Pixel yelled back.

'No, but we're going to try anyway!'
Marv smiled but inside his heart was
hammering in his chest.

They got closer, and closer, and closer until they were right behind the supervillain.

Suddenly, Master Blaster whipped around. His eyes went wide as he spotted Marv and Pixel and then he began frantically firing ice blasts in their direction.

'Now!' Marv shouted to Pixel. He leapt into the air as high as he could, somehow avoiding the ice beams. Just like his jump earlier, time seemed to slow down, but unlike before this jump was superpowered! Marv went so high that he sailed completely over Master Blaster's head.

Then, as he started dropping back towards the ice, he spun in the air, and Pixel made a leap of her own. She flung herself off Marv's shoulders and towards Master Blaster. Pixel's steel hands ripped the glowing necklace, pulling it off the supervillain's neck. Pixel hurled the necklace back to Marv.

Marv reached out as far as his arm could go and caught the necklace with his fingertips before crashing to the floor. Ice sprayed into the air as he skidded to a wobbly, but upright, stop.

Where was Pixel? Marv's first thought was for his friend. He swivelled around searching the ice.

'No!' Marv said in a quiet voice. Pixel was frozen solid at Master Blaster's feet.

Master Blaster huffed and puffed, his face red with anger. He lifted up his arm, once again aiming straight at Marv.

CHAPTER 6

Master Blaster thrust his hand forward. Marv closed his eyes tight waiting for the ice blast, but nothing happened. He opened his eyes. Master Blaster was pushing his hand forward over and over again, but nothing was coming out.

Marv looked around. All the
penguins had stopped moving. They had
turned back to their usual plastic selves.

Marv looked down at the necklace
in his hand. They'd been right. Without
the crystal, Master Blaster's powers had
gone!

'Give me my necklace
back, right now!' Master
Blaster shouted. He
stomped his skates
angrily but stopped

when that movement made him wobble and nearly lose his balance. 'If you don't give it back to me right now—' Master Blaster slipped on the ice, but just managed to keep himself upright. He could barely move on the ice any more.

He was no threat!

'Have fun skating, Master Blaster. I've got some work to do,' Marv said.

'De-freeze blast, please activate!' Marv said, putting his hand over the suit's 'M' symbol. A large vent in his suit's arm opened and he unfroze Pixel.

'Did we do it?' Pixel chirped the moment she was free.

'Yeah, we did it. Thanks to you, Pixel.' Marv grinned. 'Do you know how to turn this off?' he said, handing the glowing crystal over to the robot.

'No! Don't!' Master Blaster yelled, but Marv and Pixel ignored him.

'All sidekicks have a 'Mysterious Crystals' section in our handbooks. I read mine pretty recently so . . .' Pixel trailed off. A bunch of lights suddenly projected out of Pixel's eyes, quickly scanning over the crystal. In a few seconds, the crystal had stopped glowing. 'It should be turned off now and it won't be possible to use it again.'

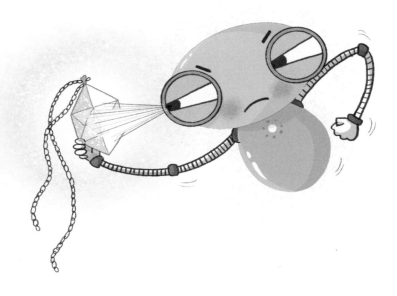

Marv grinned. Master Blaster groaned.

'Well, Master Blaster, now you'll have to enjoy the ice rink just like the rest of us,' Marv said, as Master Blaster stumbled off the ice.

Marv glanced around at all of the frozen people. 'Let's get unfreezing, Pixel.'

Pixel nodded. 'I estimate that ninety per cent of the unfrozen people will freak out if we don't fix some of the chaos around here.'

Marv glanced around. Pixel was right. All the ice blasting had created a total disaster zone. There was a whole bunch of hot dogs all over the floor, a couple of speakers had icy holes in them, and the rubbish bins had been completely turned over.

'I'll sort this mess out while you unfreeze people,' Pixel said.

Marv nodded. 'OK. Let's meet up when we're done.'

Marv got to work. He skated all
around the ice rink using his heat steam
to unfreeze everyone who had been
frozen by Master Blaster.

The strangest thing was, that when people were unfrozen they just went on with whatever they were doing before Master Blaster arrived. It was like they had been pulled out from a trance and didn't remember anything of what had just happened. Soon, the sounds of laughter and talking filled the arena once again.

Eventually, Marv reached his grandad. He gently used his heat steam to unfreeze him. Chunks of ice slowly fell away until his grandad was back to normal.

'Oh, look it's the superhero Marv. Hey Marv, what's the emergency?' Grandad said, with an inquisitive look on his face.

'Nothing for you to worry about,' Marv replied, and then he looked around to make sure no one was listening and whispered, 'Grandad!'

Grandad pulled his glasses down and winked. He lifted his cup of hot chocolate to his lips, then made a face. 'Hmm, that got cold fast.'

'I got it!' Marv leant forward and used the steam vent to reheat the hot chocolate.

'Ooo, thanks!' Grandad grinned.

Marv got back onto the ice and looked around. Everything was back to normal. No one seemed to know that a supervillain had just been here, well no one except for Eva and Joe.

'Marv!' Eva cried out as she and Joe tentatively skated over.

'Thanks for saving the day again, Marv.' Joe grinned.

'I'm just glad I could help,' Marv said in a muffled way, trying to disguise his voice.

Eva stepped forward. 'Can you please help us with one more thing? We have a friend called Marvin. He came to the ice rink too, but we haven't seen him since the attack by that supervillain. He's probably frozen somewhere, can you check?'

'Yes, I'll look for him now,' Marv said. He knew that this was probably the cue for him to get out of his super-suit.

'Thank you, Marv,' Eva and Joe said at the same time.

Marv hurried off to the edge of the ice rink. He went straight over to his backpack, where he found Pixel waiting for him. Then he quickly ran to the bathroom and changed out of his super-suit—transforming from Marv the superhero back to Marvin the boy again.

Marvin was ready to head out onto the ice, but he knew he couldn't leave Pixel behind this time. Pixel really was an awesome sidekick and Marvin didn't know how he would have defeated Master Blaster without her.

'Pixel, I'm really really sorry for leaving you out of all the fun earlier. I wouldn't be a superhero if it wasn't for you,' Marvin said, with his head down. He found it hard to meet Pixel's eyes.

'And I wouldn't be a sidekick if it wasn't for you,' Pixel replied. 'I'm glad I could help. And in the end, I did get to go out onto the ice!'

'Do you want to come skating now? You'd need to stay hidden, but you could ride around in my backpack?' Marvin asked.

'I think I've had enough ice for one day. I'll sit by Grandad and keep him company,' she said.

'We really do need each other, don't we?' Marvin looked at Pixel and smiled.

'Yes, together we have the most powerful superpower of all.' Pixel smiled back.

'Friendship!' Marvin replied.

'High five!' Pixel and Marvin high fived, laughing.

Pixel jumped back into Marvin's backpack and he dropped her off with his grandad before heading back to the ice.

'Hey, Marvin! You're OK!' Joe cried.

'Yeah, you missed it! A supervillain attacked the ice rink and Marv saved the day,' Eva said, talking excitedly.

'That sounds so cool. I wish I'd got to see it,' Marvin said with a knowing grin.

'Don't worry, we can tell you all about it while we ice skate,' Joe said.

'Wait,' Marvin began, nervously. 'I just wanted to say that I'm sorry for earlier, for rushing off and leaving you both

behind. I was being a show-off and I'm
sorry. Are we still friends?'

Joe and Eva smiled. 'Of course we're
still friends,' Eva said, wrapping her arms
around Marvin and Joe's shoulders.

'Yeah, of course we are,' Joe added.

The sound of someone clearing their

throat came from behind the group.
Marvin and his friends turned around. It
was Ally and the older kids.

'You're pretty good on the ice,
Marvin. Why don't you come skate with
us?' Ally asked. 'Those two can't keep
up,' she pointed at Eva and Joe, 'but you
can.'

'Thanks, but no thanks,' Marvin said without even a little bit of hesitation. 'I'm happy hanging out over here, with my friends.'

The older kids skated away and Marvin, Joe, and Eva looked at each other with giant grins on their faces. This was what a visit to the ice rink was all about.

Marvin skated back and forth across the ice, jumping into the air and trying that 360 degree spin again and again. Without his super-suit, he couldn't land it without falling over.

Joe kept losing control of his penguin, slipping and sliding across the ice.

Eva fell over onto her bum every five minutes.

At one point they were all on the floor, looking at each other and laughing.

It was the most fun Marvin could remember having in ages.

ABOUT THE AUTHOR

ALEX FALASE-KOYA

Alex is a London native. He has been writing children's fiction since he was a teenager and was a winner of Spread the Word's 2019 London Writers Awards for YA and Children's. He co-wrote *The Breakfast Club Adventures*, the first fiction book by Marcus Rashford. He now lives in Walthamstow with his girlfriend and two cats.

ABOUT THE ILLUSTRATOR

PAULA BOWLES

Paula grew up in Hertfordshire, and has
always loved drawing, reading, and using
her imagination, so she studied illustration
at Falmouth College of Arts and became an
illustrator. She now lives in Bristol, and has
worked as an illustrator for over ten years, and
has had books published with Nosy Crow and
Simon & Schuster.

MARV

Marvin's life changed when he found an old superhero suit and became MARV. The suit has been passed down through Marvin's family and was last worn by his grandad. It's powered by the kindness and imagination of the wearer and doesn't work for just anybody.

COURAGE	7
FRIENDSHIP	9
KINDNESS	9
POWERS	10
AGILITY	7
COMBAT SKILLS	6

PIXEL

PIXEL is Marv's brave superhero sidekick. Her quick thinking and unwavering loyalty make her the perfect crime-fighting companion.

COURAGE	6
FRIENDSHIP	10
KINDNESS	9
POWERS	5
AGILITY	7
COMBAT SKILLS	5

MASTER BLASTER

MASTER BLASTER is a villian with ice powers. His skating ability paired with his power to shoot ice blasts make him a deadly foe. However, all his power comes from one magical object that can be destroyed.

COURAGE	5
FRIENDSHIP	3
KINDNESS	3
POWERS	8
AGILITY	8
COMBAT SKILLS	7

'THE SUPER-SUIT IS POWERED BY TWO THINGS: **KINDNESS** AND **IMAGINATION.** LUCKILY YOU, MARVIN, HAVE TONS OF BOTH!'

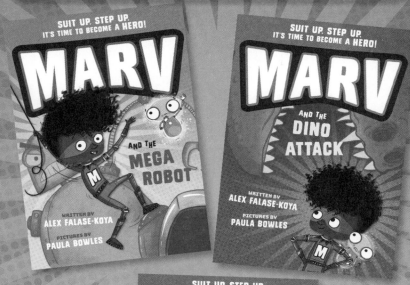

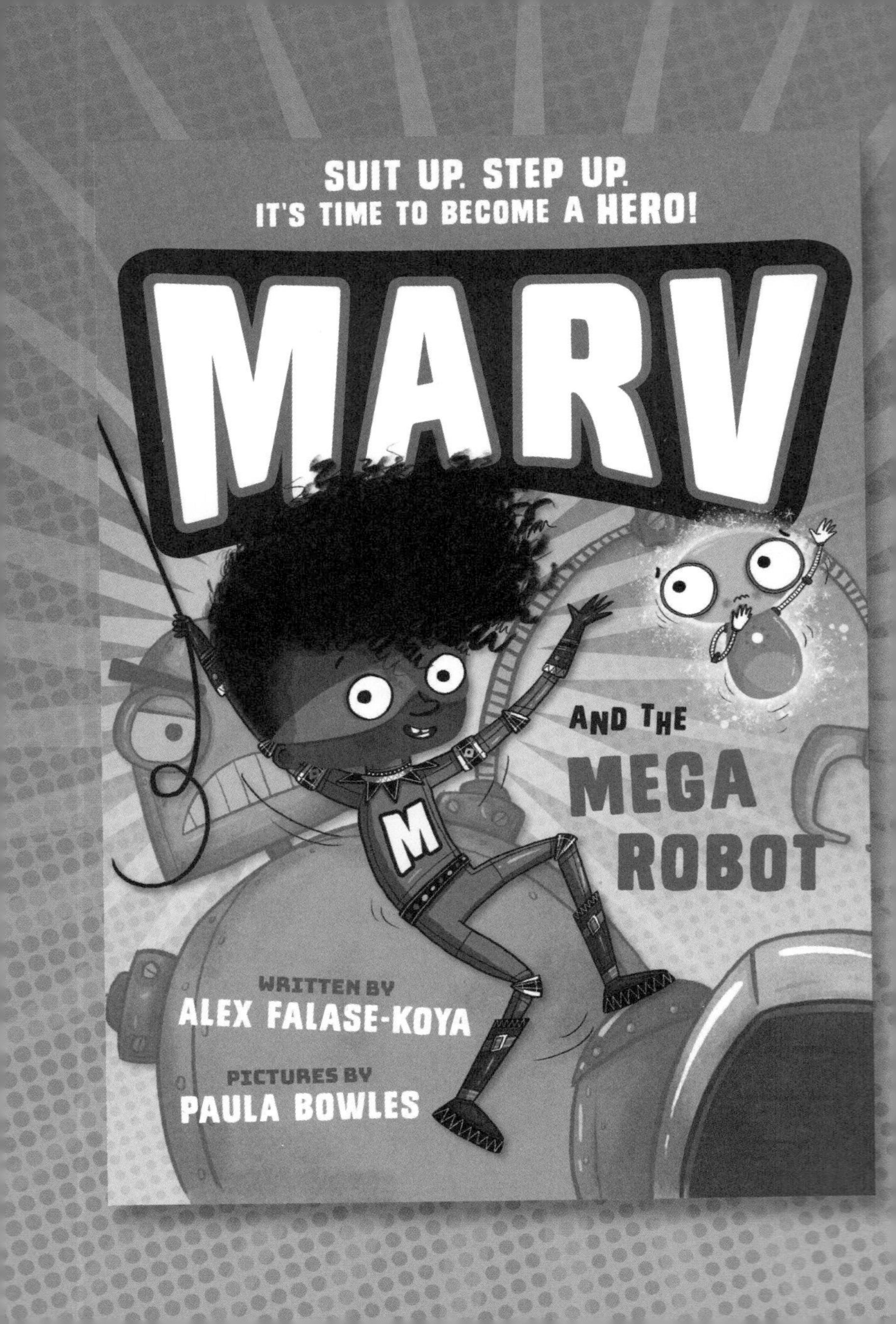
SUIT UP. STEP UP.
IT'S TIME TO BECOME A HERO!
MARV
AND THE
MEGA
ROBOT
M
WRITTEN BY
ALEX FALASE-KOYA
PICTURES BY
PAULA BOWLES

'THE SUPER-SUIT IS POWERED BY TWO THINGS: KINDNESS AND IMAGINATION. LUCKILY YOU, MARVIN, HAVE TONS OF BOTH!'

Marvin loves reading about superheroes and now he's about to become one for real.

Grandad is passing his superhero suit and robot sidekick, Pixel, on to Marvin. It's been a long time since the world needed a superhero but now, with a mega robot and a supervillain on the loose, that time has come.

To defeat his enemies and protect his friends, Marvin must learn to trust the superhero within. Only then will Marvin become MARV – unstoppable, invincible, and **totally marvellous!**

LOVE MARV?
WHY NOT TRY THESE TOO...?

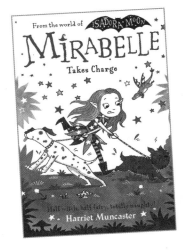